55671 EN
Lunch Box

P9-CFA-491

Maccarone, Grace
ATOS BL 1.2
Points: 0.5   LG

A NOTE TO PARENTS

Reading Aloud with Your Child

Research shows that reading books aloud is the single most valuable support parents can provide in helping children learn to read.

- Be a ham! The more enthusiasm you display, the more your child will enjoy the book.
- Run your finger underneath the words as you read to signal that the print carries the story.
- Leave time for examining the illustrations more closely; encourage your child to find things in the pictures.
- Invite your youngster to join in whenever there's a repeated phrase in the text.
- Link up events in the book with similar events in your child's life.
- If your child asks a question, stop and answer it. The book can be a means to learning more about your child's thoughts.

Listening to Your Child Read Aloud

The support of your attention and praise is absolutely crucial to your child's continuing efforts to learn to read.

- If your child is learning to read and asks for a word, give it immediately so that the meaning of the story is not interrupted. DO NOT ask your child to sound out the word.
- On the other hand, if your child initiates the act of sounding out, don't intervene.
- If your child is reading along and makes what is called a miscue, listen for the sense of the miscue. If the word "road" is substituted for the word "street," for instance, no meaning is lost. Don't stop the reading for a correction.
- If the miscue makes no sense (for example, "horse" for "house"), ask your child to reread the sentence because you're not sure you understand what's just been read.
- Above all else, enjoy your child's growing command of print and make sure you give lots of praise. *You are your child's first teacher — and the most important one. Praise from you is critical for further risk-taking and learning.*

— Priscilla Lynch
Ph.D., New York University
Educational Consultant

To Betsy Molisani—Thanks
for the lunch!
— G.M.

To Angie "Nana" Cosentino
—B.L.

Text copyright © 1995 by Grace Maccarone.
Illustrations copyright © 1995 by Betsy Lewin.
All rights reserved. Published by Scholastic Inc.
HELLO READER!, CARTWHEEL BOOKS, and the CARTWHEEL BOOKS
logo are registered trademarks of Scholastic Inc.

Library of Congress Cataloging-in-Publication Data

Maccarone, Grace.
    The lunch box surprise / by Grace Maccarone ; illustrated by Betsy Lewin.
        p.   cm. — (First grade friends ; bk. 1) (Hello reader! Level 1)
    "Cartwheel Books."
    Summary: When Sam's mother forgets to pack his lunch, his friends in the
first grade come to his rescue.
    ISBN 0-590-26267-X
    [1. Schools — Fiction.   2. Friendship — Fiction.]   I. Lewin, Betsy, ill.
II. Title.   III. Series.   IV. Series: Maccarone, Grace. First grade friends ;
bk. 1.
PZ7.M1257Lu   1995   95-10284
[E]—dc20   CIP
                                                                            AC

12 11 10 9 8 7   7 8 9/9 0/0

First Scholastic printing, September 1995

The Lunch Box Surprise

by Grace Maccarone
Illustrated by Betsy Lewin

Hello Reader! — Level 1

Cartwheel
B·O·O·K·S ®

SCHOLASTIC INC.
New York Toronto London Auckland Sydney

"It's time for lunch.
It's time to eat,"
the teacher says.
"Now take your seat!"

"My lunch is best," say Jan and Pam

and Kim and Dan

and Max and Sam.

Jan has peanut butter,
bread, and jam.

Pam has soup.

Dan has ham.

Kim has tuna,
toast, and cheese.

Max has chicken,
rice, and peas.

But Sam has nothing—
not a spot.
Sam has nothing!
His mom forgot!

Sam is surprised.
Sam is sad.
Sam is hungry.
Sam is mad!

But Max and Kim,
Jan, Dan, and Pam
feel sorry
for their sad friend, Sam.

Jan gives Sam
peanut butter,
bread, and jam.

Pam gives him soup.
Dan gives him ham.

Kim gives him tuna,
toast, and cheese.

Max gives him chicken,
rice, and peas.

Now Sam is not sad
and Sam is not mad.
This is the best lunch
Sam ever had!